3 1994 01406 7422

10/08

SANTA ANA PUBLIC LIBRARY
NEWHOPE BRANCH

AR PTS: 0.5

D0603934

J FICTION PARKER, J.
Parker, Jeff *SUPERHEROES*
Fantastic Four in His *PARK*
    latest flame

                              $21.35
        NEW HOPE   31994014067422

IRRADIATED BY COSMIC RAYS AND TRANSFORMED TO POSSESS SUPERHUMAN POWERS, THEY JOINED TOGETHER TO FIGHT EVIL. **MISTER FANTASTIC,** THE **INVISIBLE WOMAN,** THE **HUMAN TORCH** AND THE **THING.** TOGETHER THEY CALL THEMSELVES THE **FANTASTIC FOUR** IN

HIS LATEST FLAME

| JEFF PARKER | JUAN SANTACRUZ | RAUL FERNANDEZ | SOTOCOLOR'S A. CROSSLEY | DAVE SHARPE |
| WRITER | PENCILS | INKS | COLORS | LETTERS |

RYAN, MORALES and HOLLOWELL — COVER
JAMES TAVERAS — PRODUCTION
NATHAN COSBY — ASST. EDITOR
NICOLE WILEY — EDITOR
CADENHEAD and PANICCIA — CONSULTING EDITORS
JOE QUESADA — CHIEF
DAN BUCKLEY — PUBLISHER

MARVEL

Spotlight

VISIT US AT
www.abdopublishing.com

Spotlight library bound edition © 2007. Spotlight is a division of ABDO Publishing Company, Edina, Minnesota.

MARVEL, and all related character names and the distinctive likenesses thereof are trademarks of Marvel Characters, Inc., and is/are used with permission. Copyright © 2006 Marvel Characters, Inc. All rights reserved. www.marvel.com

MARVEL, Fantastic Four: TM & © 2006 Marvel Characters, Inc. All rights reserved. www.marvel.com. This book is produced under license from Marvel Characters, Inc.

Cataloging Data

Parker, Jeff
    Fantastic Four in his latest flame / Jeff Parker, writer ; Juan Santacruz, pencils ; Raul Fernandez, inks. -- Library bound ed.
        p. cm. -- (Fantastic Four)
    Summary: Irradiated by cosmic rays and transformed to possess superhuman powers, Mr. Fantastic, the Invisible Woman, the Human Torch, and the Thing join together to fight evil.
    "Marvel age"--Cover.
    Revision of the November 2005 issue of Marvel adventures Fantastic Four.
    ISBN-13: 978-1-59961-201-0
    ISBN-10: 1-59961-201-1
    1. Fantastic Four (Fictitious characters)--Comic books, strips, etc.--Fiction. 2. Graphic novels. I. Title. II. Title: His latest flame   III. Series.

741.5dc22

All Spotlight books are reinforced library binding
and manufactured in the United States of America

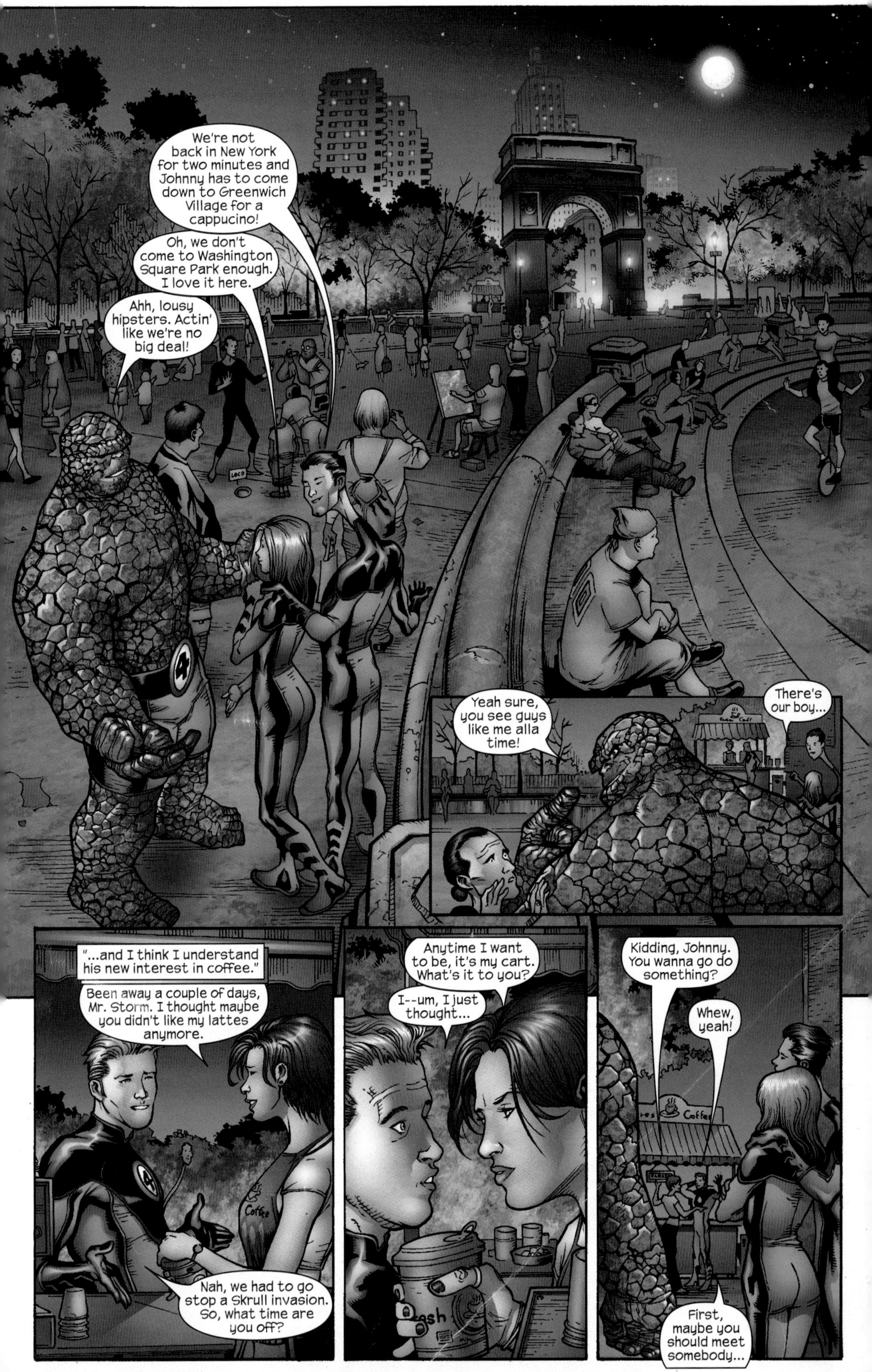
We're not back in New York for two minutes and Johnny has to come down to Greenwich Village for a cappucino!
Oh, we don't come to Washington Square Park enough. I love it here.
Ahh, lousy hipsters. Actin' like we're no big deal!
Yeah sure, you see guys like me alla time!
There's our boy...
"...and I think I understand his new interest in coffee."
Been away a couple of days, Mr. Storm. I thought maybe you didn't like my lattes anymore.
Nah, we had to go stop a Skrull invasion. So, what time are you off?
Anytime I want to be, it's my cart. What's it to you?
I--um, I just thought...
Kidding, Johnny. You wanna go do something?
Whew, yeah!
First, maybe you should meet somebody...

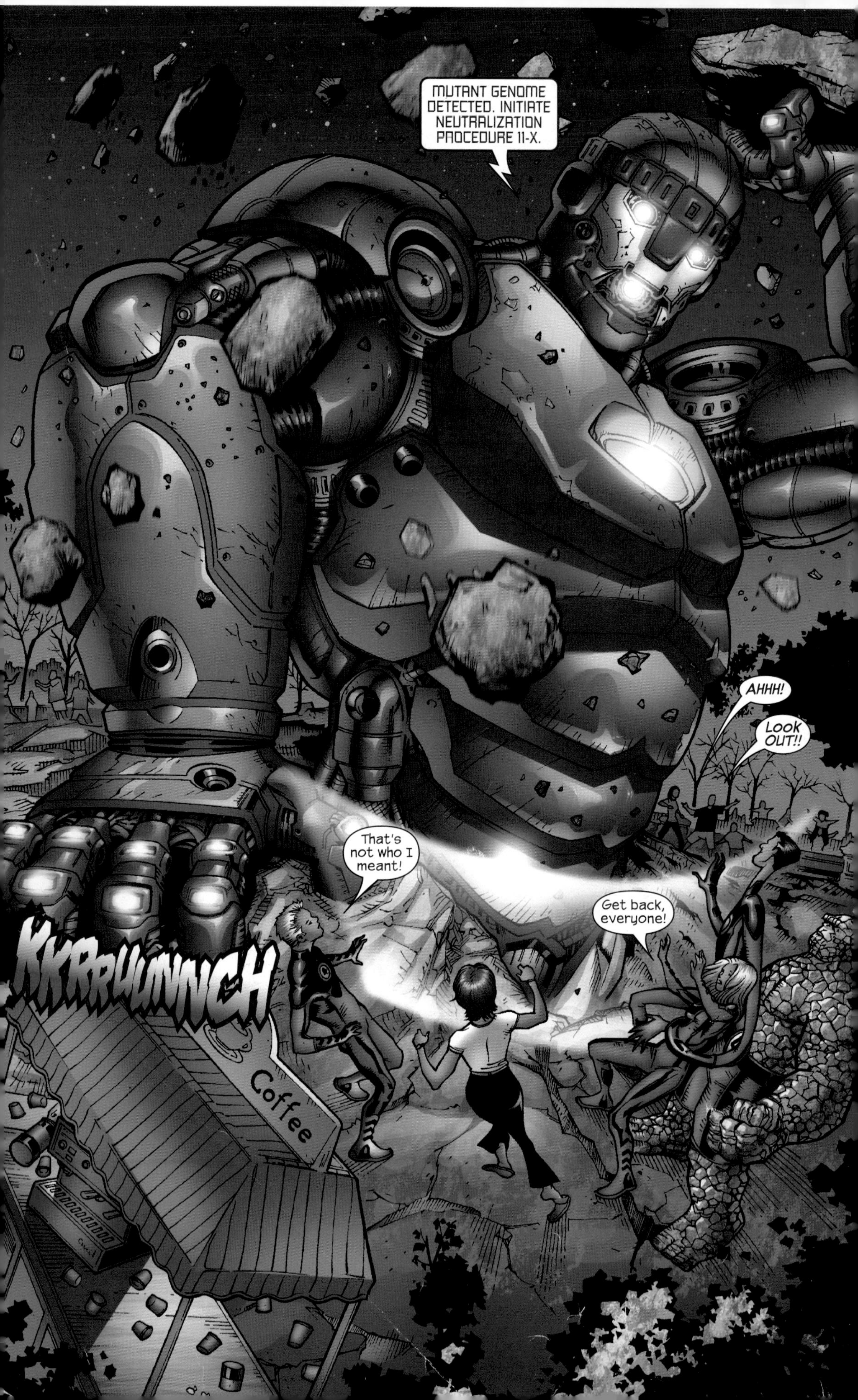
MUTANT GENOME DETECTED. INITIATE NEUTRALIZATION PROCEDURE 11-X.
AHHH!
LOOK OUT!!
That's not who I meant!
Get back, everyone!
KKRRUUNNCH
Coffee

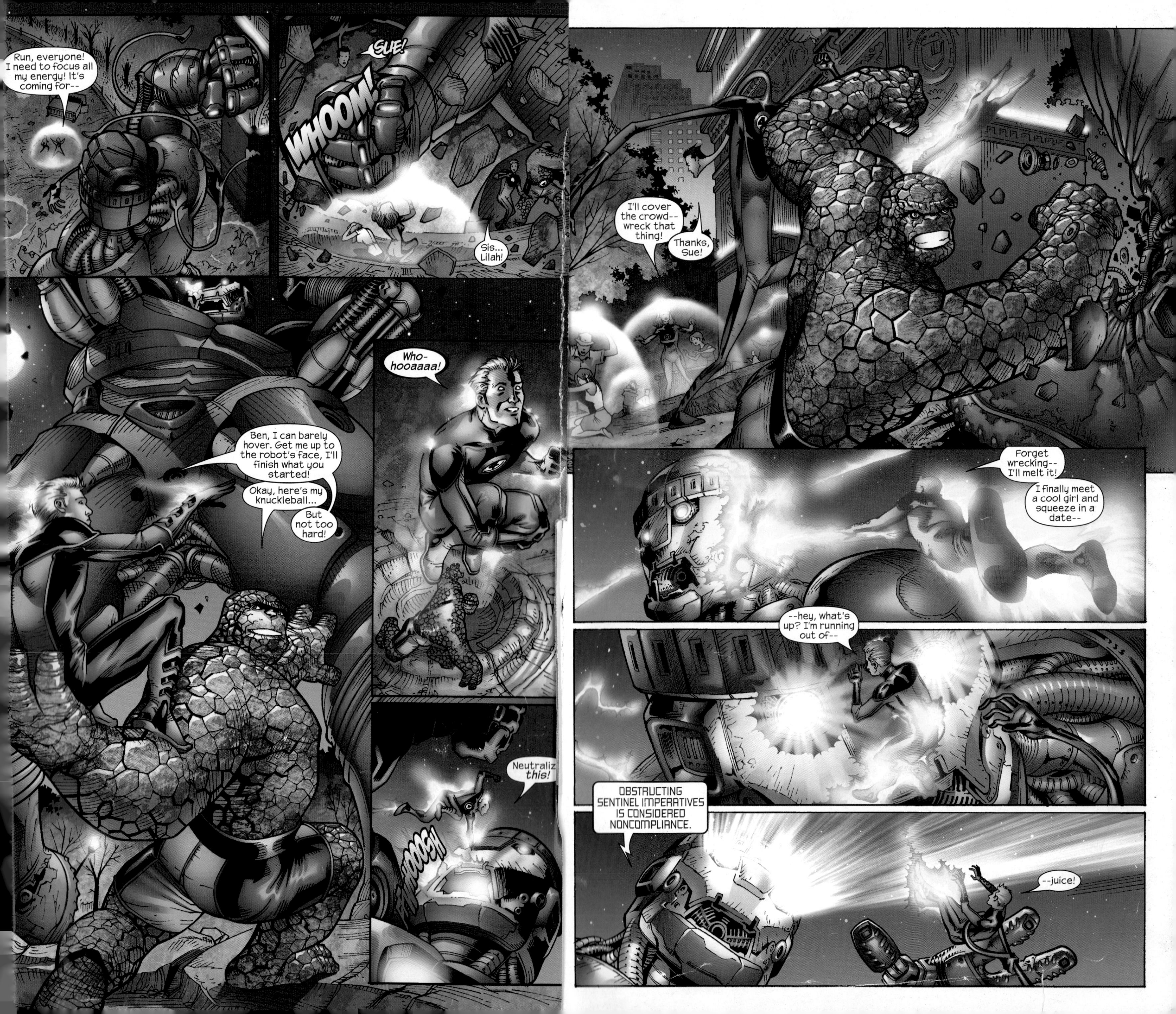
Run, everyone! I need to focus all my energy! It's coming for--
SUE!
WHOOM!
Sis... Lilah!
Ben, I can barely hover. Get me up to the robot's face, I'll finish what you started!
Okay, here's my knuckleball...
But not too hard!
Who-hooaaaa!
Neutraliz this!
I'll cover the crowd-- wreck that thing!
Thanks, Sue!
Forget wrecking-- I'll melt it!
I finally meet a cool girl and squeeze in a date--
--hey, what's up? I'm running out of--
OBSTRUCTING SENTINEL IMPERATIVES IS CONSIDERED NONCOMPLIANCE.
--juice!

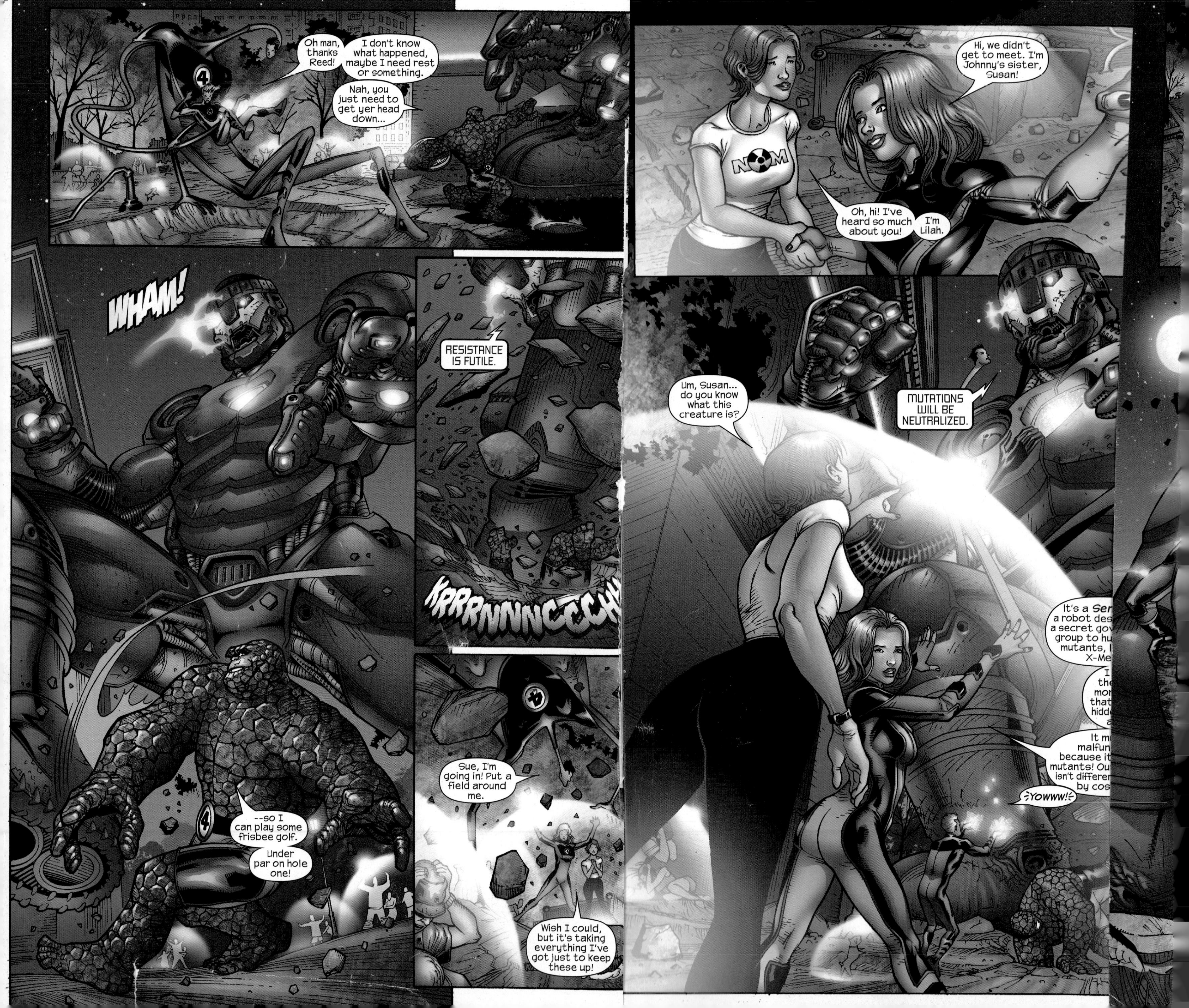
Oh man, thanks Reed!
I don't know what happened, maybe I need rest or something.
Nah, you just need to get yer head down...
WHAM!
RESISTANCE IS FUTILE.
KRRRNNNNCCCH
--so I can play some frisbee golf.
Under par on hole one!
Sue, I'm going in! Put a field around me.
Wish I could, but it's taking everything I've got just to keep these up!
Hi, we didn't get to meet. I'm Johnny's sister, Susan!
Oh, hi! I've heard so much about you!
I'm Lilah.
Um, Susan... do you know what this creature is?
MUTATIONS WILL BE NEUTRALIZED.
YOWWW!

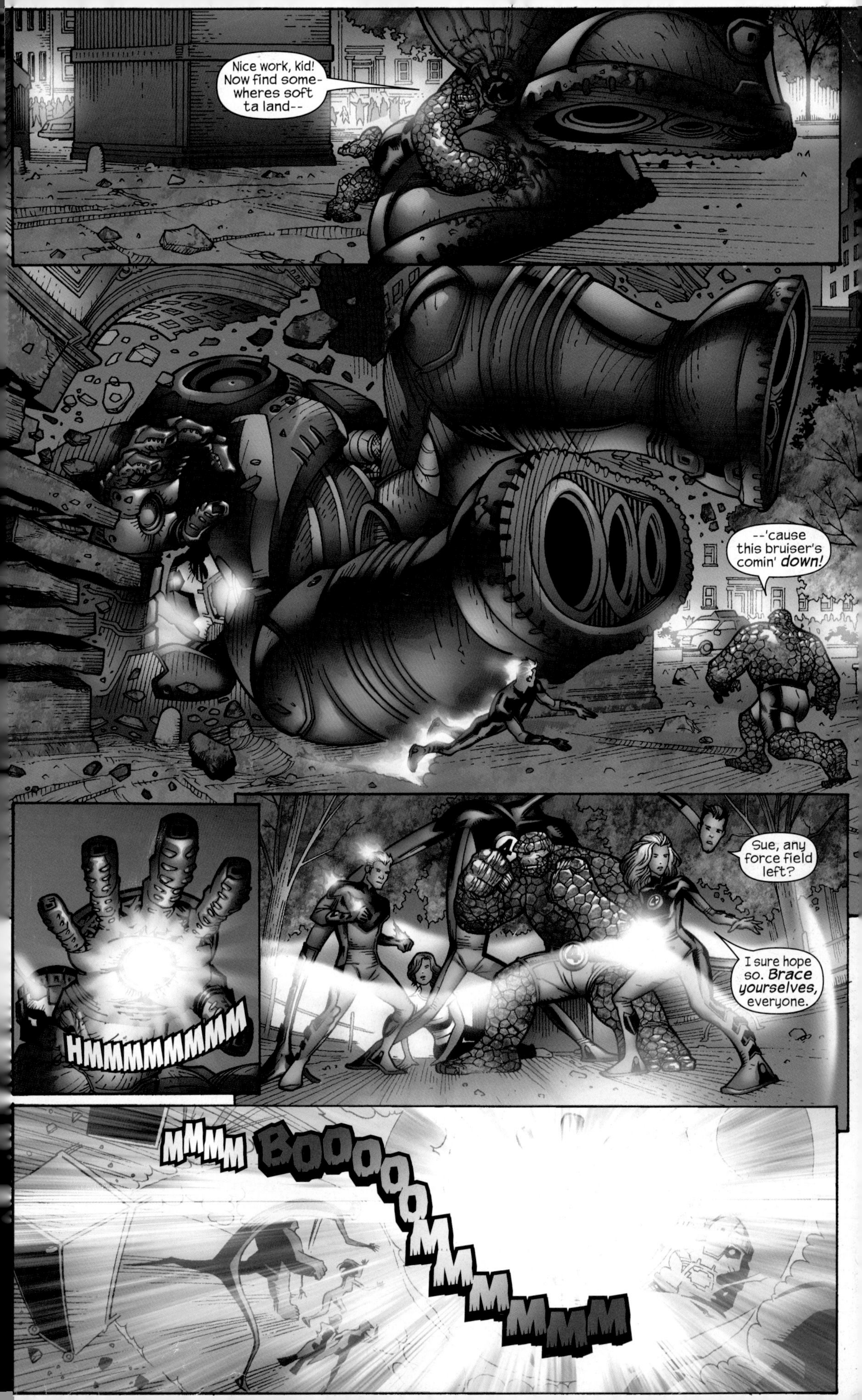
Nice work, kid! Now find some-wheres soft ta land--
--'cause this bruiser's comin' *down!*
HMMMMMMMMM
Sue, any force field left?
I sure hope so. *Brace yourselves,* everyone.
MMMM BOOOOOOMMMMMMMM

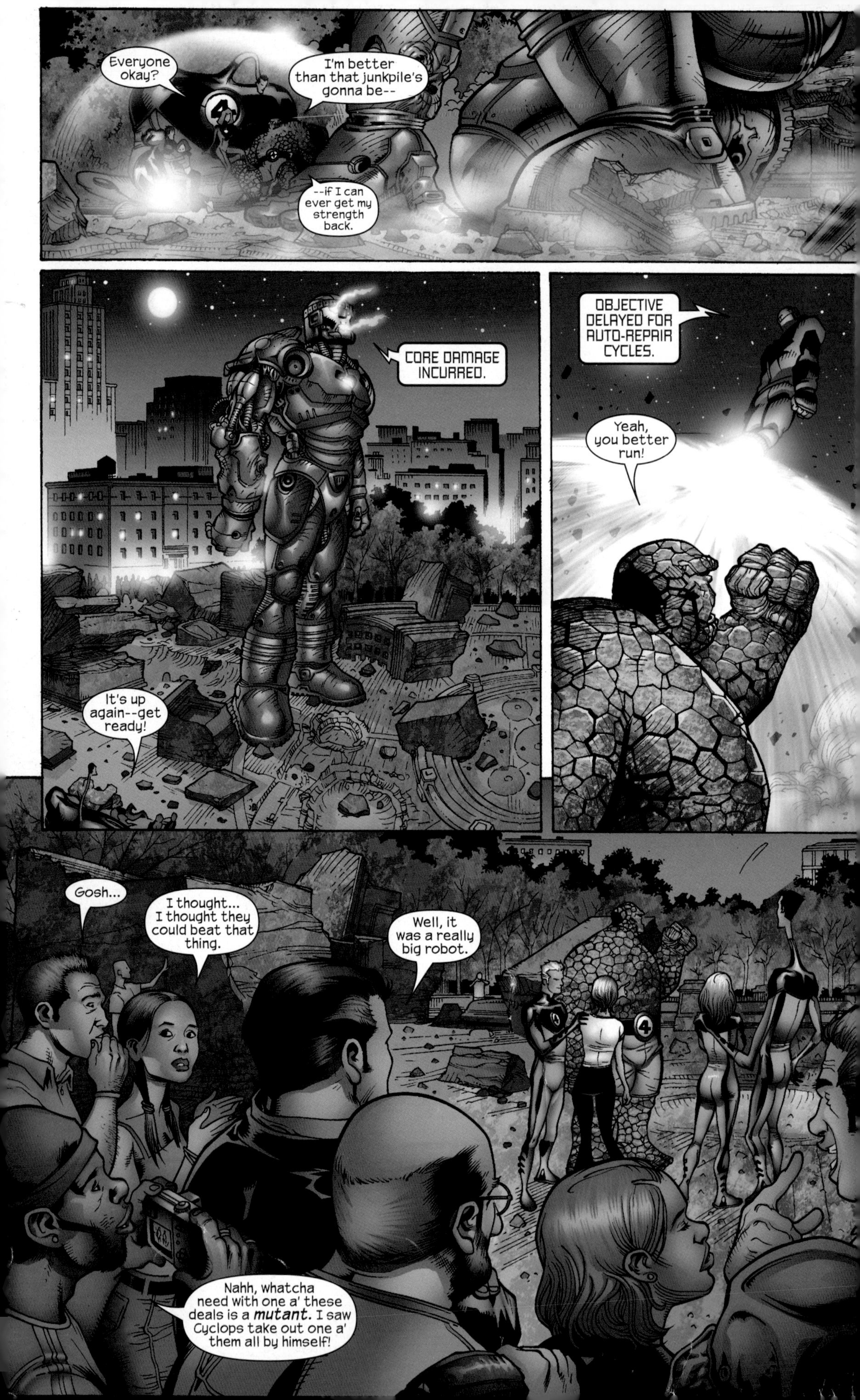
Everyone okay?
I'm better than that junkpile's gonna be--
--if I can ever get my strength back.
CORE DAMAGE INCURRED.
It's up again--get ready!
OBJECTIVE DELAYED FOR AUTO-REPAIR CYCLES.
Yeah, you better run!
Gosh...
I thought... I thought they could beat that thing.
Well, it was a really big robot.
Nahh, whatcha need with one a' these deals is a *mutant.* I saw Cyclops take out one a' them all by himself!

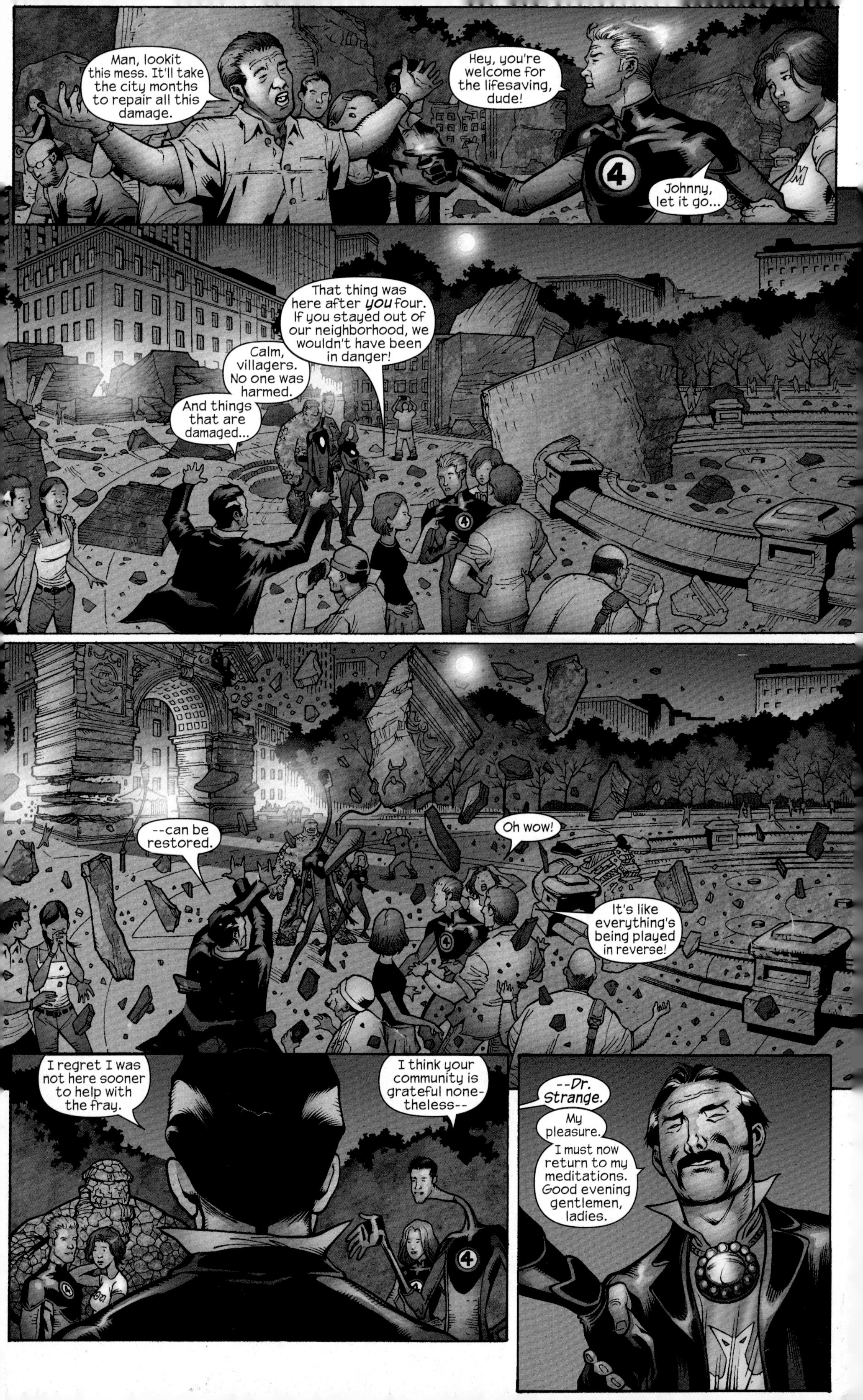
Man, lookit this mess. It'll take the city months to repair all this damage.
Hey, you're welcome for the lifesaving, dude!
Johnny, let it go...
That thing was here after YOU four. If you stayed out of our neighborhood, we wouldn't have been in danger!
Calm, villagers. No one was harmed.
And things that are damaged...
--can be restored.
Oh wow!
It's like everything's being played in reverse!
I regret I was not here sooner to help with the fray.
I think your community is grateful none-theless--
--Dr. Strange.
My pleasure.
I must now return to my meditations. Good evening gentlemen, ladies.

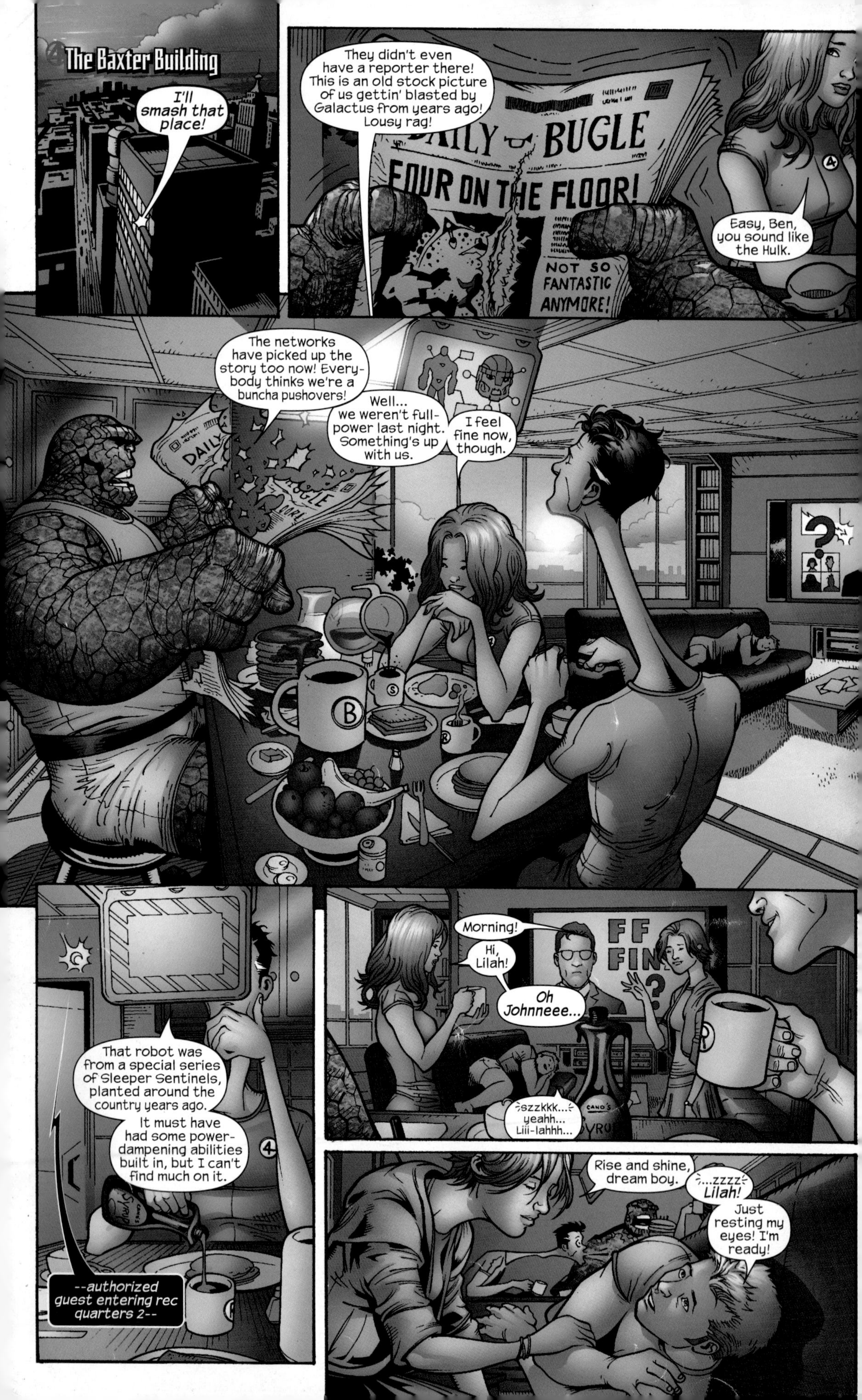
The Baxter Building
I'll smash that place!
They didn't even have a reporter there! This is an old stock picture of us gettin' blasted by Galactus from years ago! Lousy rag!
DAILY BUGLE
FOUR ON THE FLOOR!
NOT SO FANTASTIC ANYMORE!
Easy, Ben, you sound like the Hulk.
The networks have picked up the story too now! Everybody thinks we're a buncha pushovers!
Well... we weren't full-power last night. Something's up with us.
I feel fine now, though.
That robot was from a special series of Sleeper Sentinels, planted around the country years ago.
It must have had some power-dampening abilities built in, but I can't find much on it.
--authorized guest entering rec quarters 2--
Morning!
Hi, Lilah!
Oh Johnneee...
FF FIN
szzkkk... yeahh... Liii-lahhh...
Rise and shine, dream boy.
...zzzz Lilah!
Just resting my eyes! I'm ready!

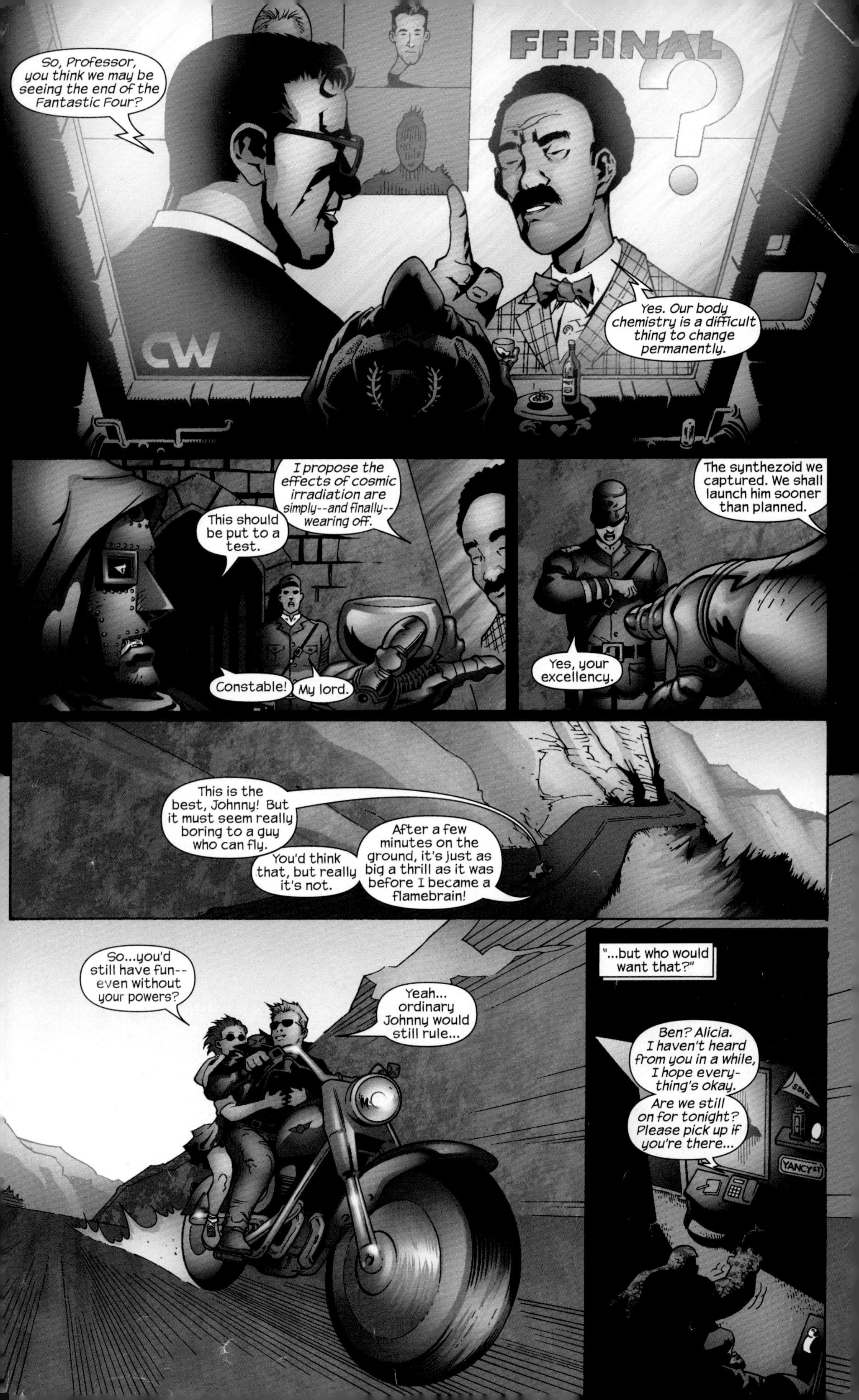
FFFINAL ?
CW
So, Professor, you think we may be seeing the end of the Fantastic Four?
Yes. Our body chemistry is a difficult thing to change permanently.
I propose the effects of cosmic irradiation are simply--and finally--wearing off.
This should be put to a test.
Constable!
My lord.
The synthezoid we captured. We shall launch him sooner than planned.
Yes, your excellency.
This is the best, Johnny! But it must seem really boring to a guy who can fly.
You'd think that, but really it's not.
After a few minutes on the ground, it's just as big a thrill as it was before I became a flamebrain!
So...you'd still have fun--even without your powers?
Yeah... ordinary Johnny would still rule...
"...but who would want that?"
Ben? Alicia. I haven't heard from you in a while, I hope every-thing's okay.
Are we still on for tonight? Please pick up if you're there...
YANCY ST

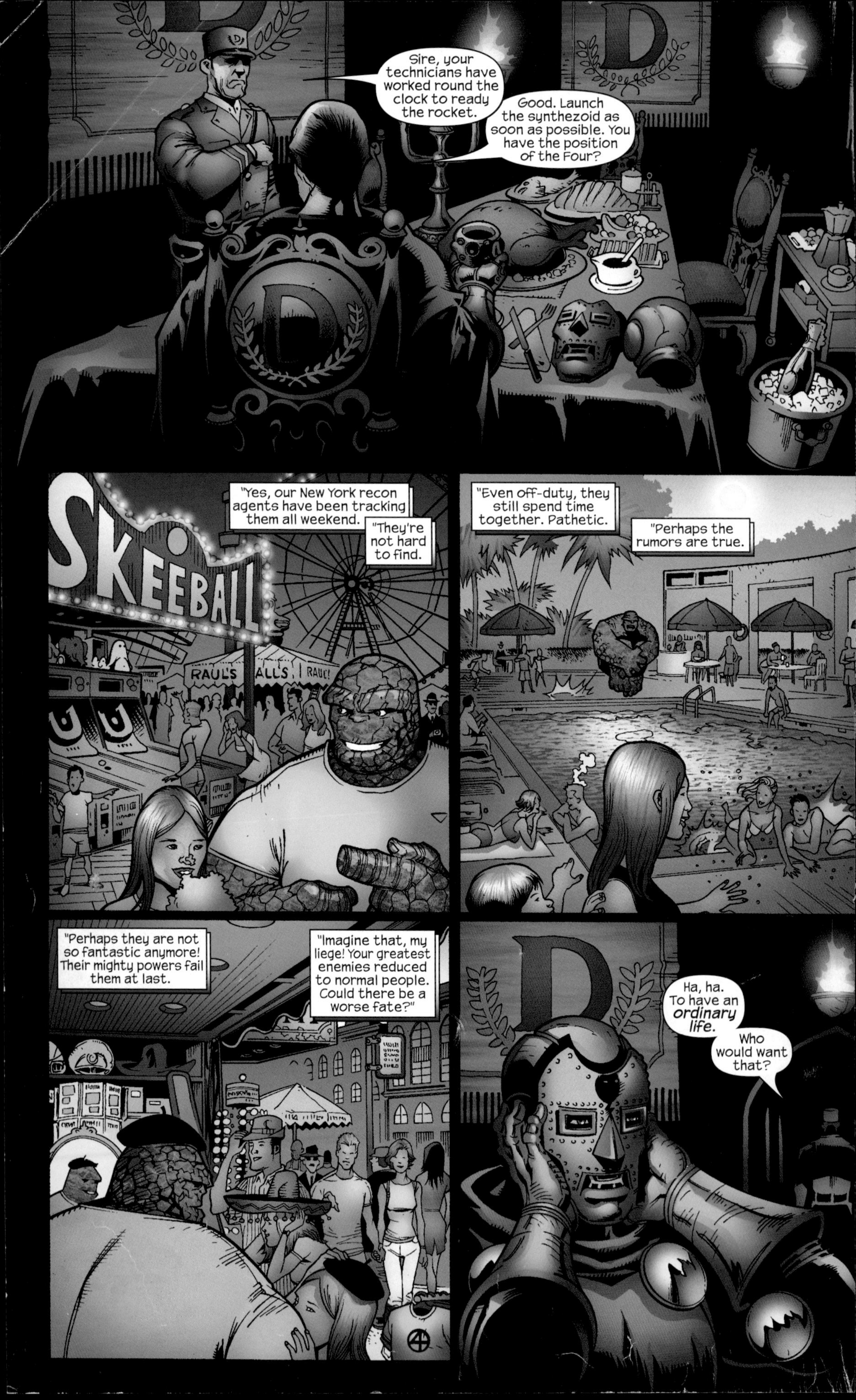
Sire, your technicians have worked round the clock to ready the rocket.
Good. Launch the synthezoid as soon as possible. You have the position of the Four?
"Yes, our New York recon agents have been tracking them all weekend.
"They're not hard to find.
SKEEBALL
RAUL'S
"Even off-duty, they still spend time together. Pathetic.
"Perhaps the rumors are true.
"Perhaps they are not so fantastic anymore! Their mighty powers fail them at last.
"Imagine that, my liege! Your greatest enemies reduced to normal people. Could there be a worse fate?"
Ha, ha. To have an *ordinary life.*
Who would want that?

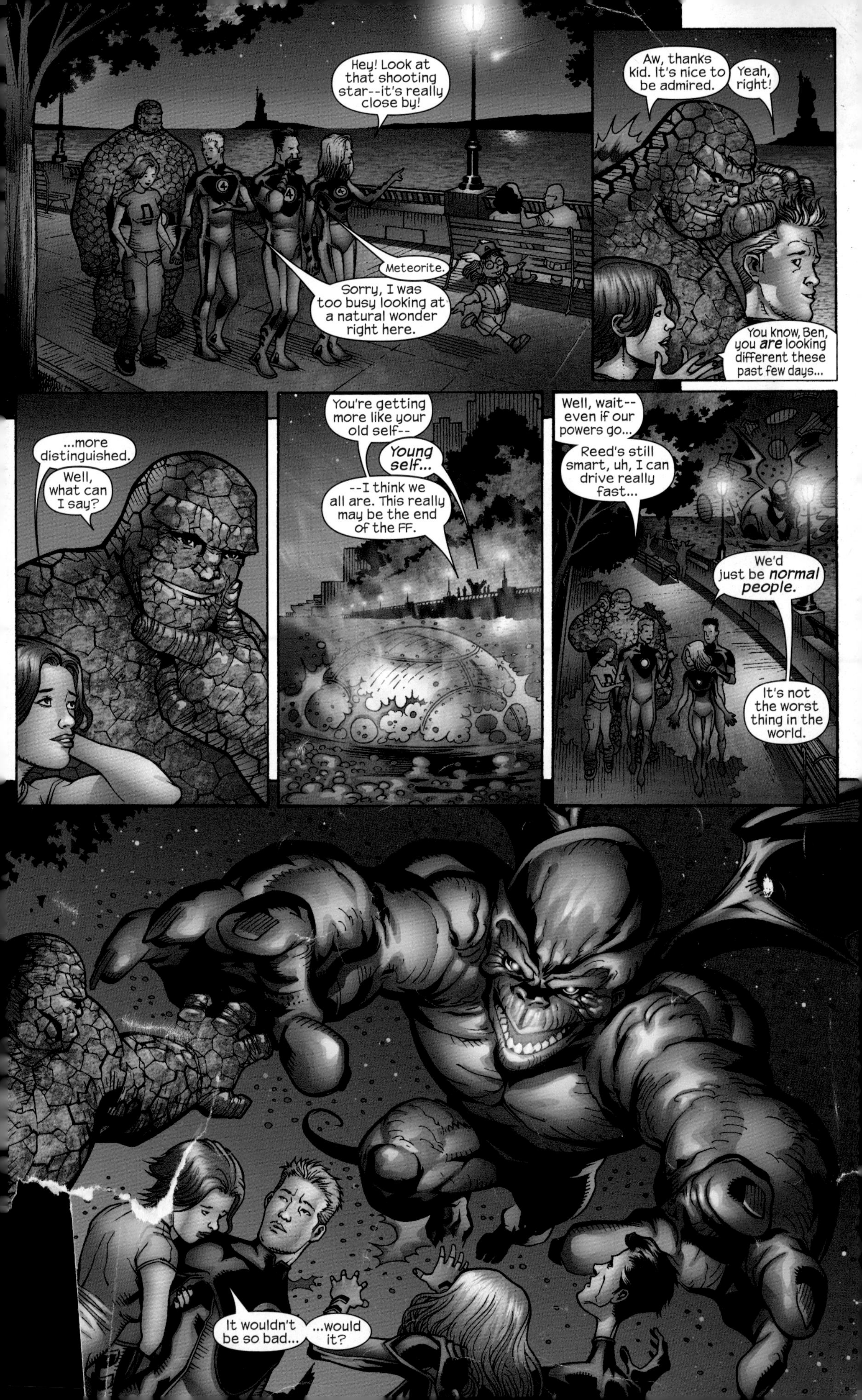
Hey! Look at that shooting star--it's really close by!
Meteorite.
Sorry, I was too busy looking at a natural wonder right here.
Aw, thanks kid. It's nice to be admired.
Yeah, right!
You know, Ben, you **are** looking different these past few days...
...more distinguished.
Well, what can I say?
You're getting more like your old self--
Young self...
--I think we all are. This really may be the end of the FF.
Well, wait--even if our powers go...
Reed's still smart, uh, I can drive really fast...
We'd just be ***normal people.***
It's not the worst thing in the world.
It wouldn't be so bad...
...would it?

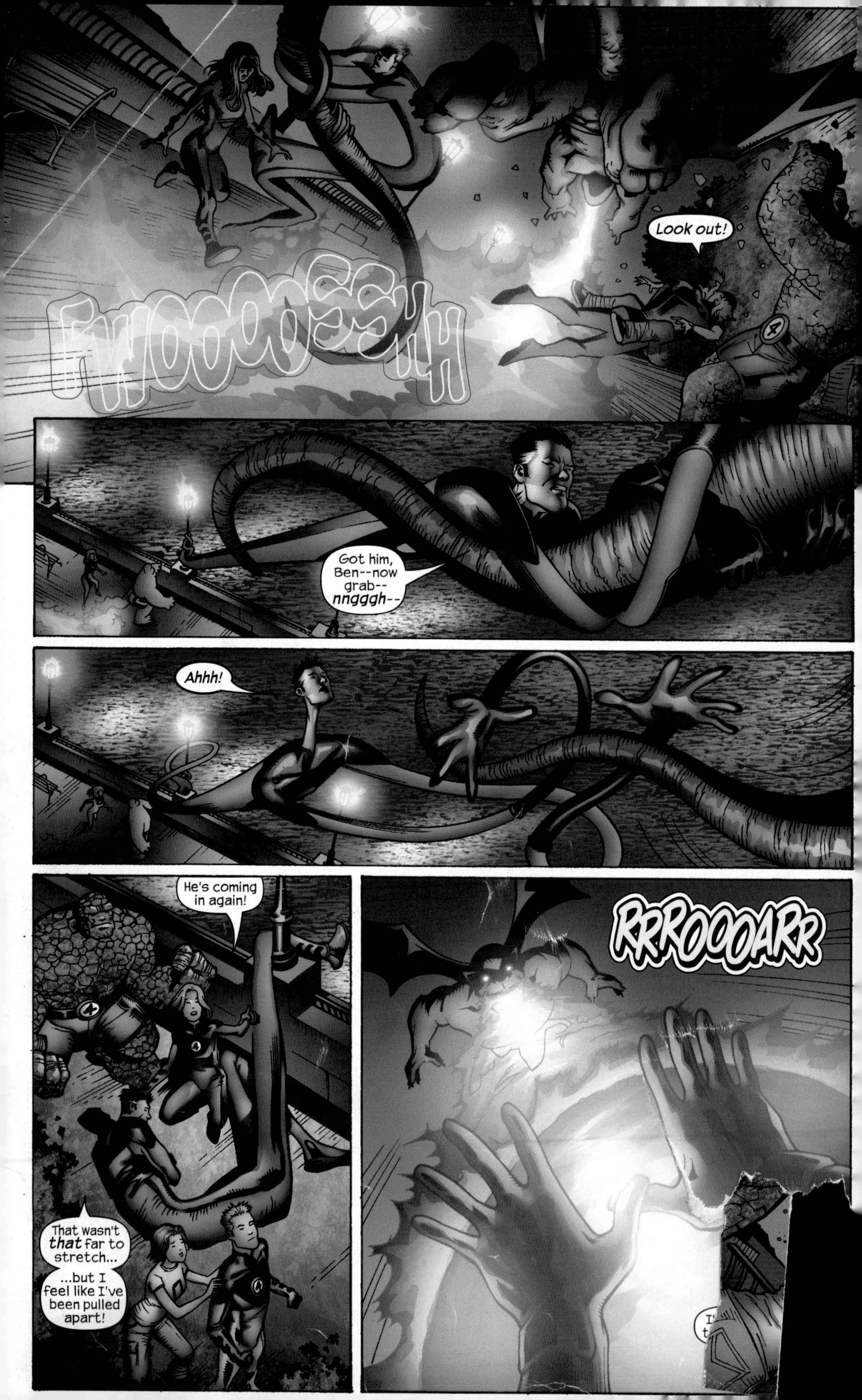
Look out!
FWOOOOSHH
Got him, Ben--now grab--nngggh--
Ahhh!
He's coming in again!
That wasn't *that* far to stretch...
...but I feel like I've been pulled apart!
RRROOOARR

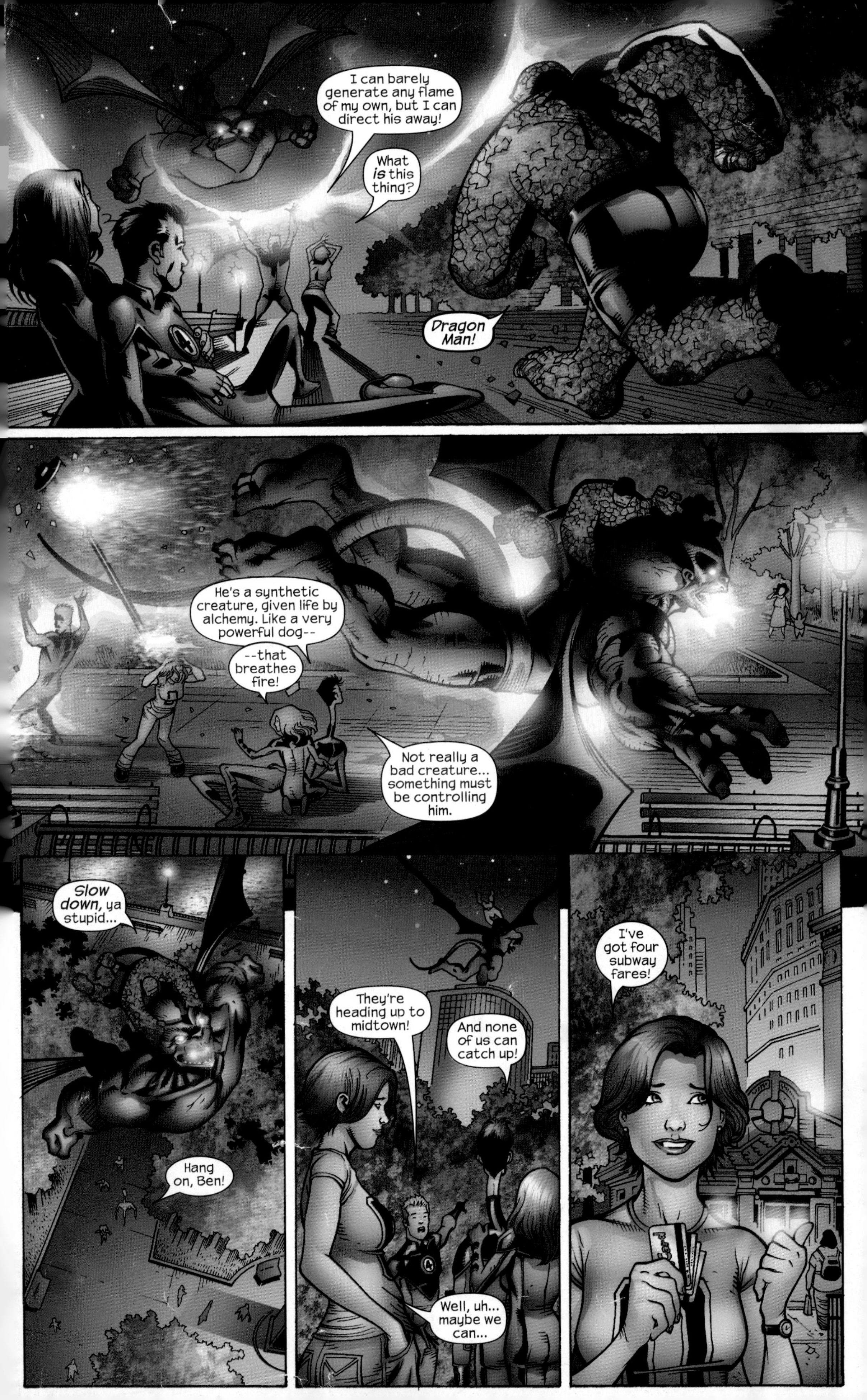

I can barely generate any flame of my own, but I can direct his away!
What *is* this thing?
Dragon Man!
He's a synthetic creature, given life by alchemy. Like a very powerful dog--
--that breathes fire!
Not really a bad creature... something must be controlling him.
Slow down, ya stupid...
Hang on, Ben!
They're heading up to midtown!
And none of us can catch up!
Well, uh... maybe we can...
I've got four subway fares!

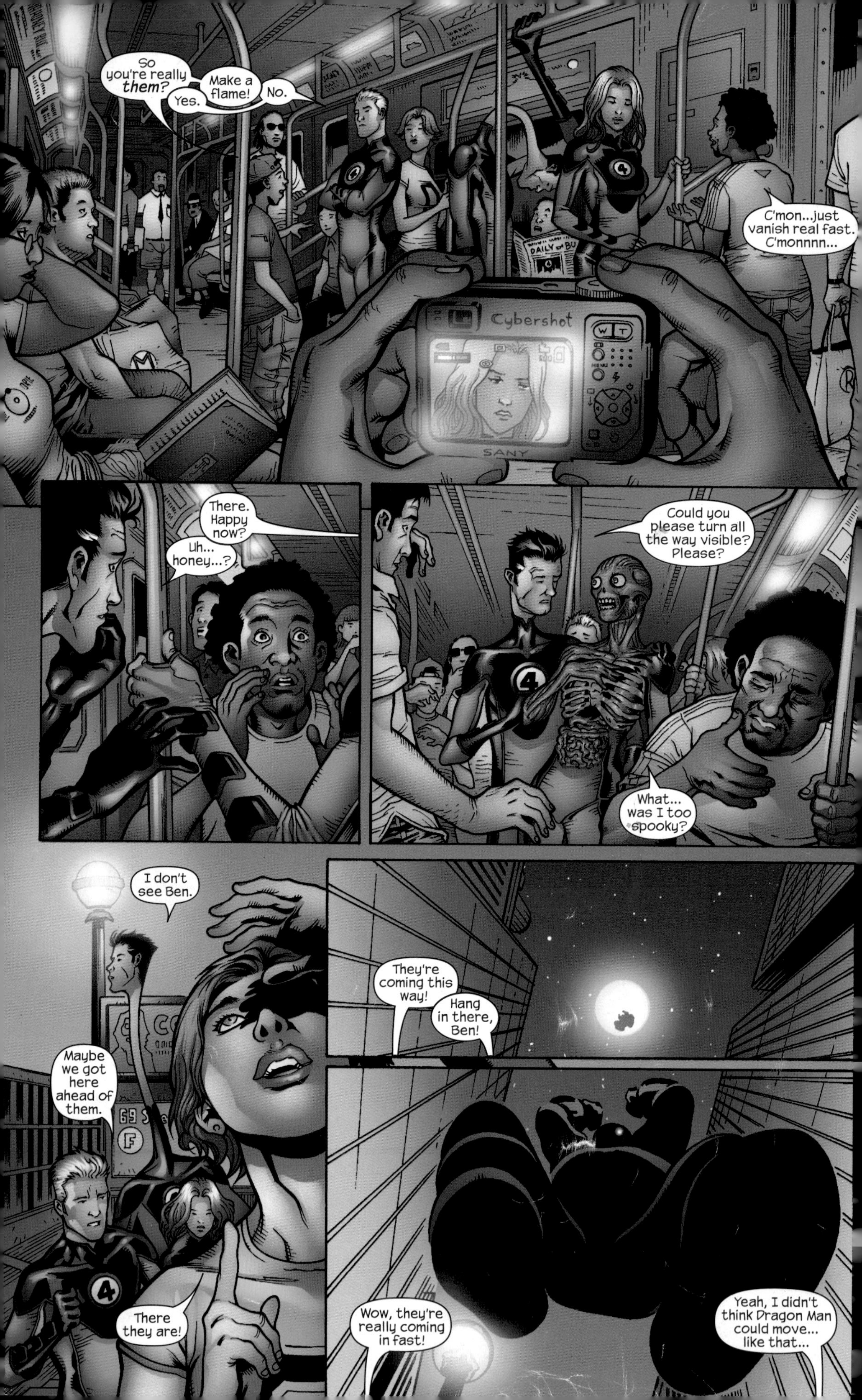
So you're really *them*?
Yes.
Make a flame!
No.
C'mon...just vanish real fast. C'monnnn...
Cybershot
There. Happy now?
Uh... honey...?
Could you please turn all the way visible? Please?
What... was I too spooky?
I don't see Ben.
Maybe we got here ahead of them.
There they are!
They're coming this way!
Hang in there, Ben!
Wow, they're really coming in fast!
Yeah, I didn't think Dragon Man could move... like that...

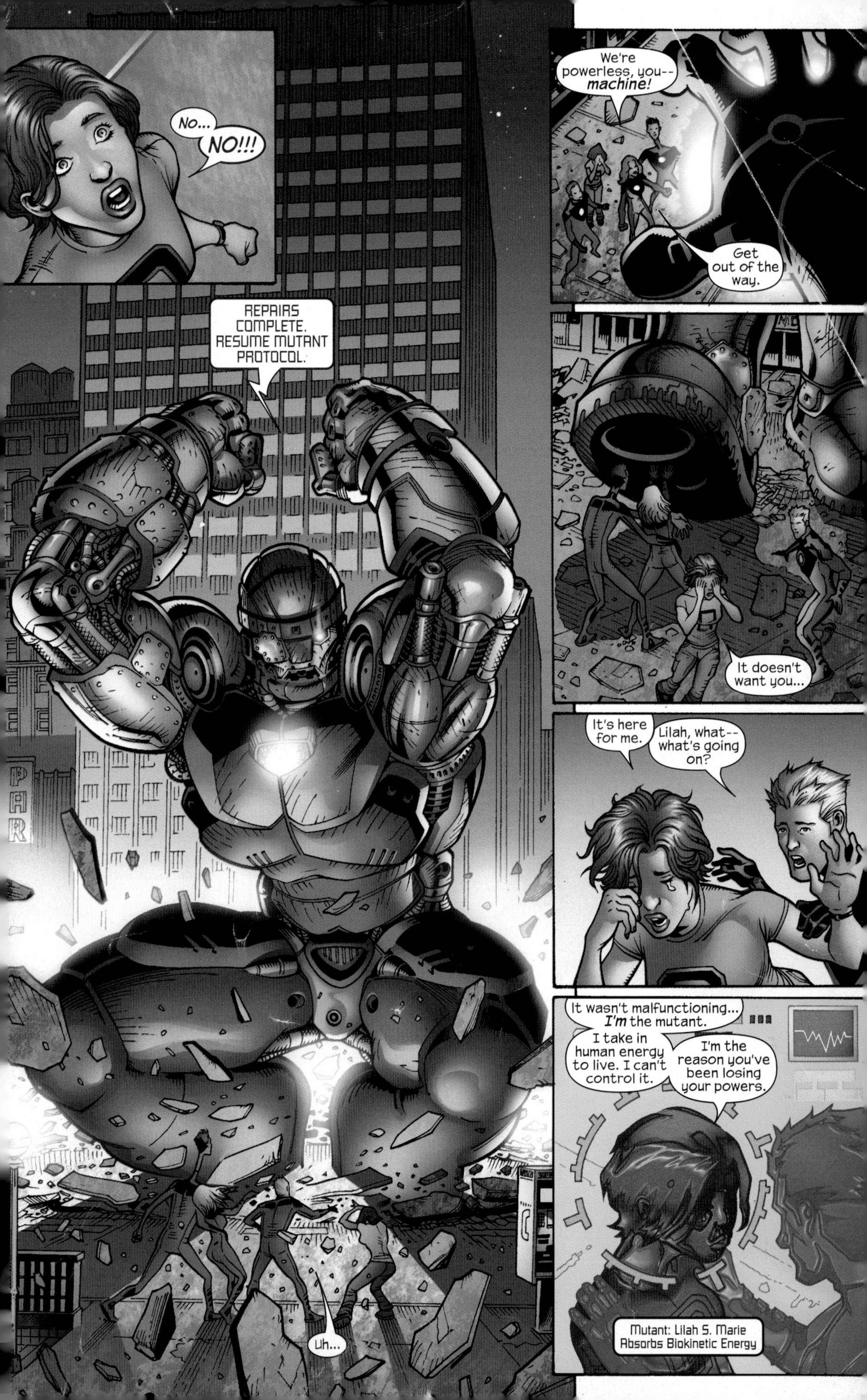
No... NO!!!
REPAIRS COMPLETE. RESUME MUTANT PROTOCOL.
Uh...
We're powerless, you-- *machine!*
Get out of the way.
It doesn't want you...
It's here for me.
Lilah, what-- what's going on?
It wasn't malfunctioning... *I'm* the mutant.
I take in human energy to live. I can't control it.
I'm the reason you've been losing your powers.
Mutant: Lilah S. Marie
Absorbs Biokinetic Energy

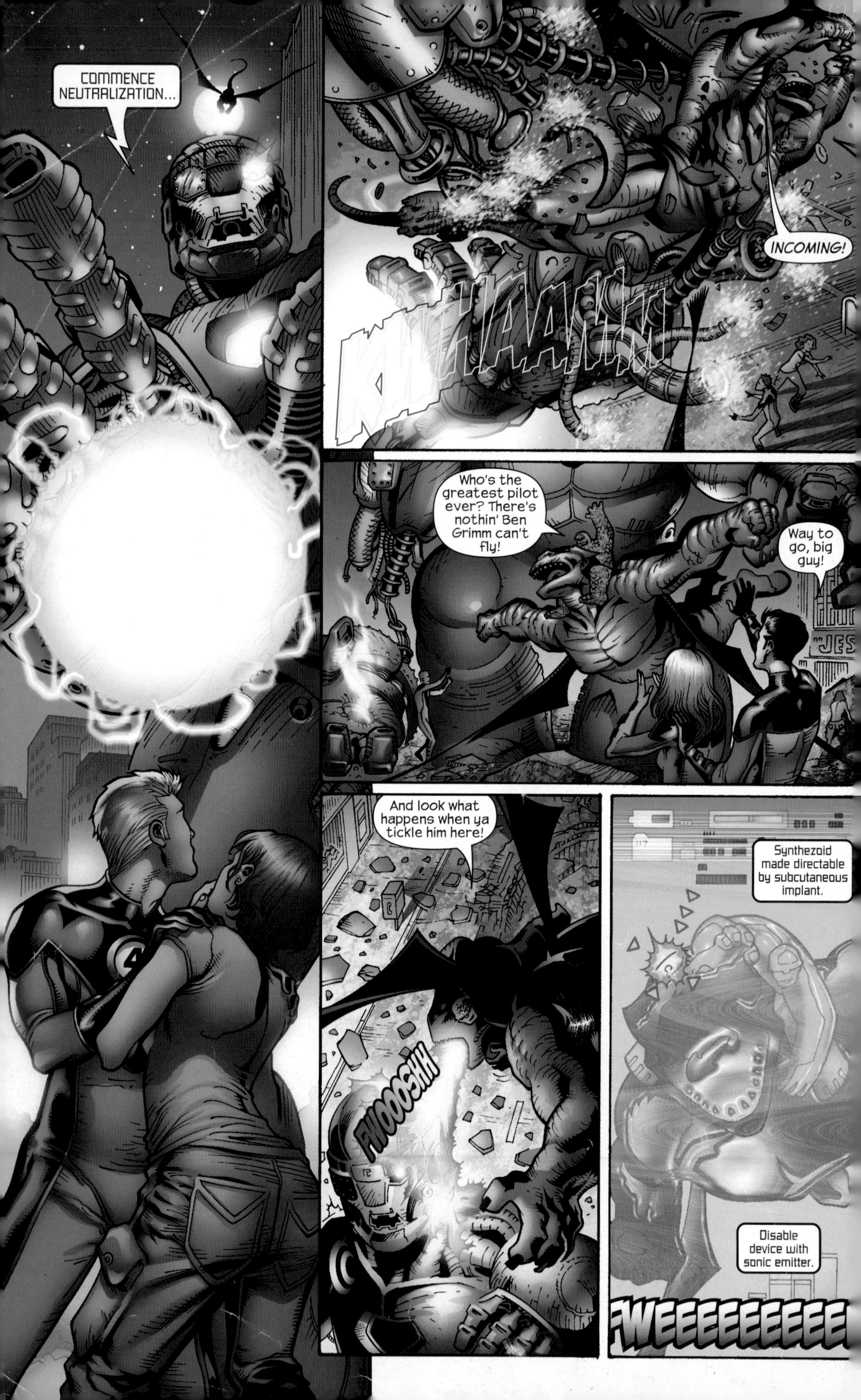
COMMENCE NEUTRALIZATION...
INCOMING!
KWHAAAMM
Who's the greatest pilot ever? There's nothin' Ben Grimm can't fly!
Way to go, big guy!
And look what happens when ya tickle him here!
FWOOOSHH
Synthezoid made directable by subcutaneous implant.
Disable device with sonic emitter.
FWEEEEEEEEE

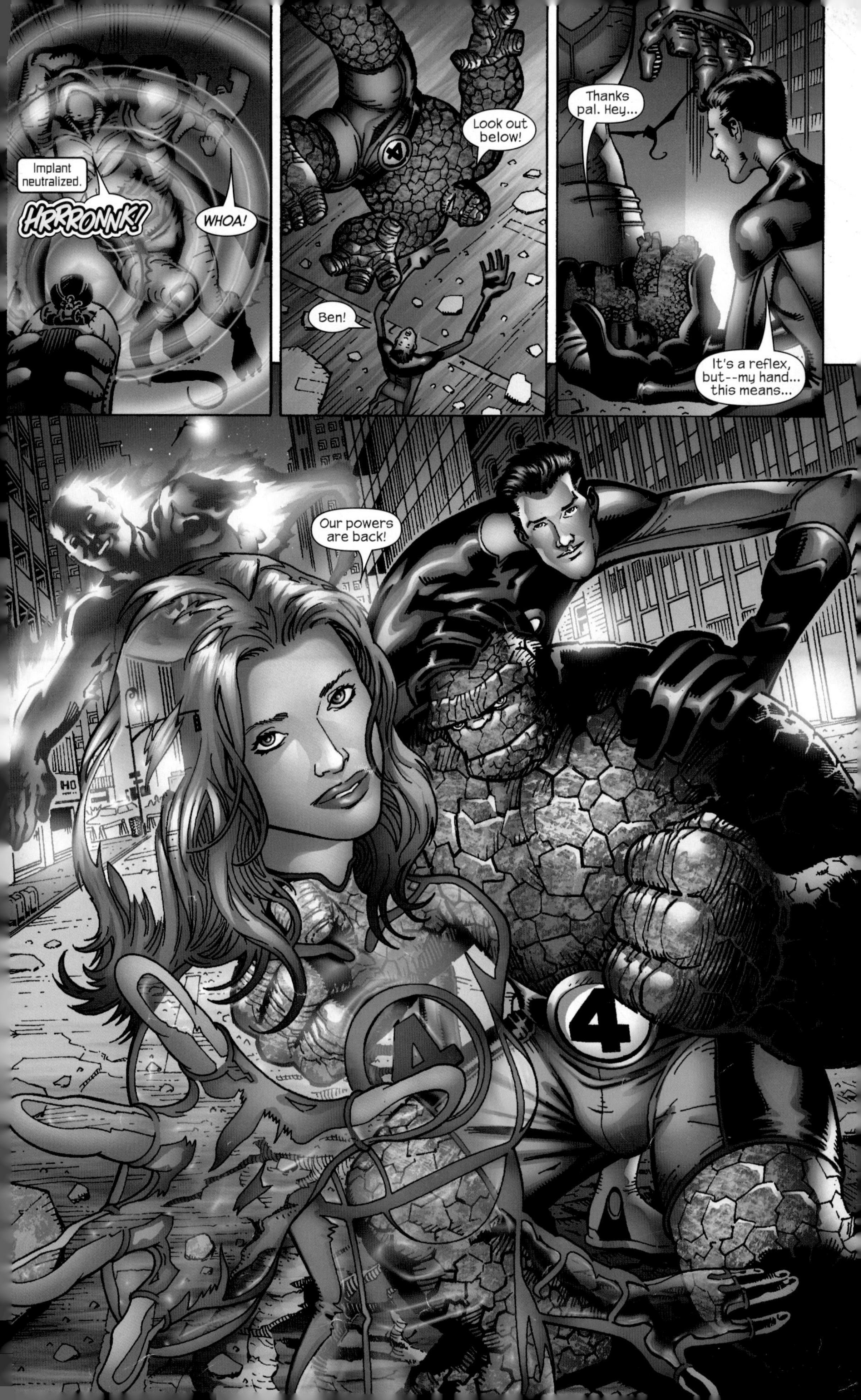
Implant neutralized.
HRRRONNK!
WHOA!
Look out below!
Ben!
Thanks pal. Hey...
It's a reflex, but--my hand... this means...
Our powers are back!

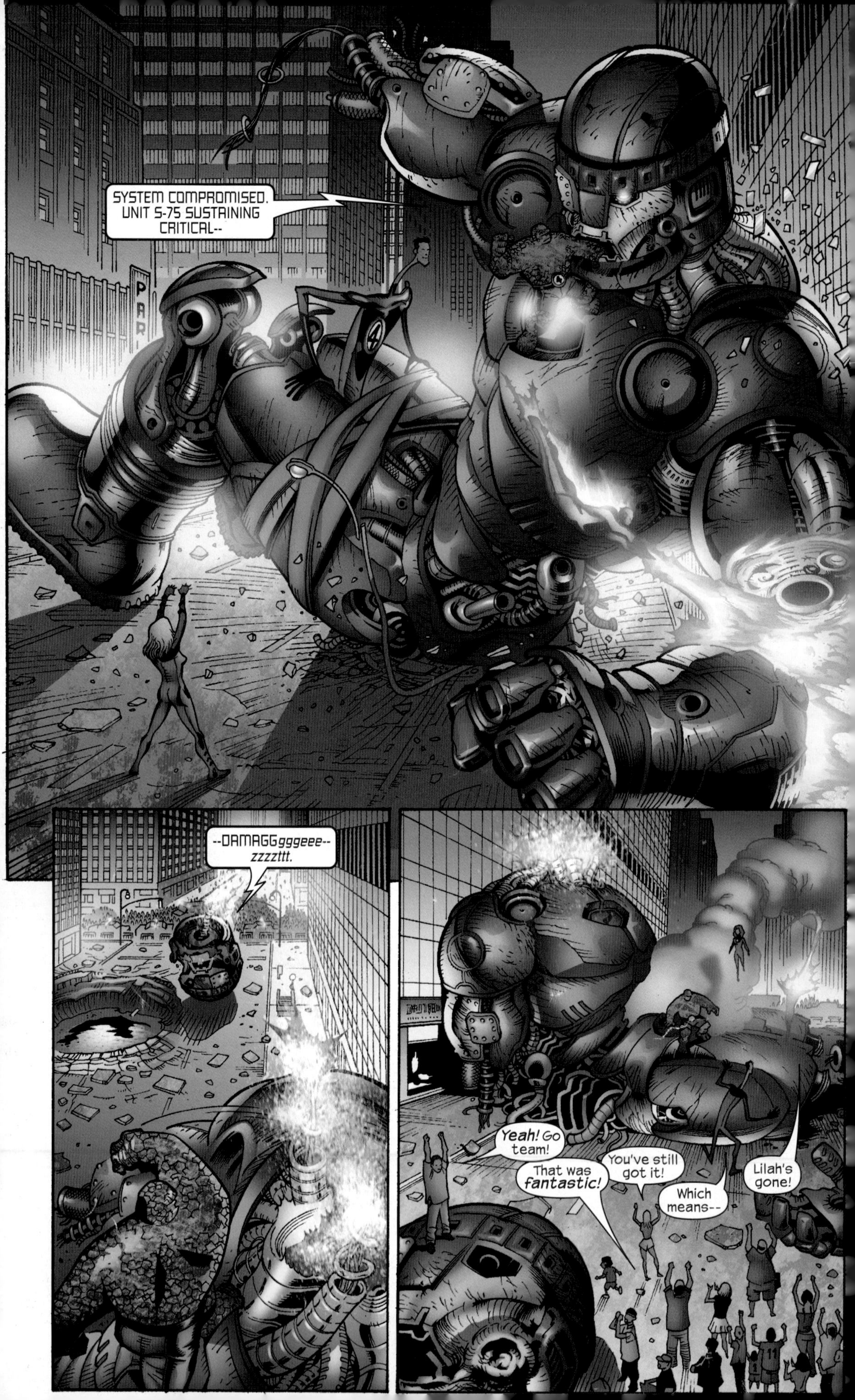
SYSTEM COMPROMISED. UNIT S-75 SUSTAINING CRITICAL--
--DAMAGGgggeee-- zzzzttt.
Yeah! Go team!
That was fantastic!
You've still got it!
Which means--
Lilah's gone!

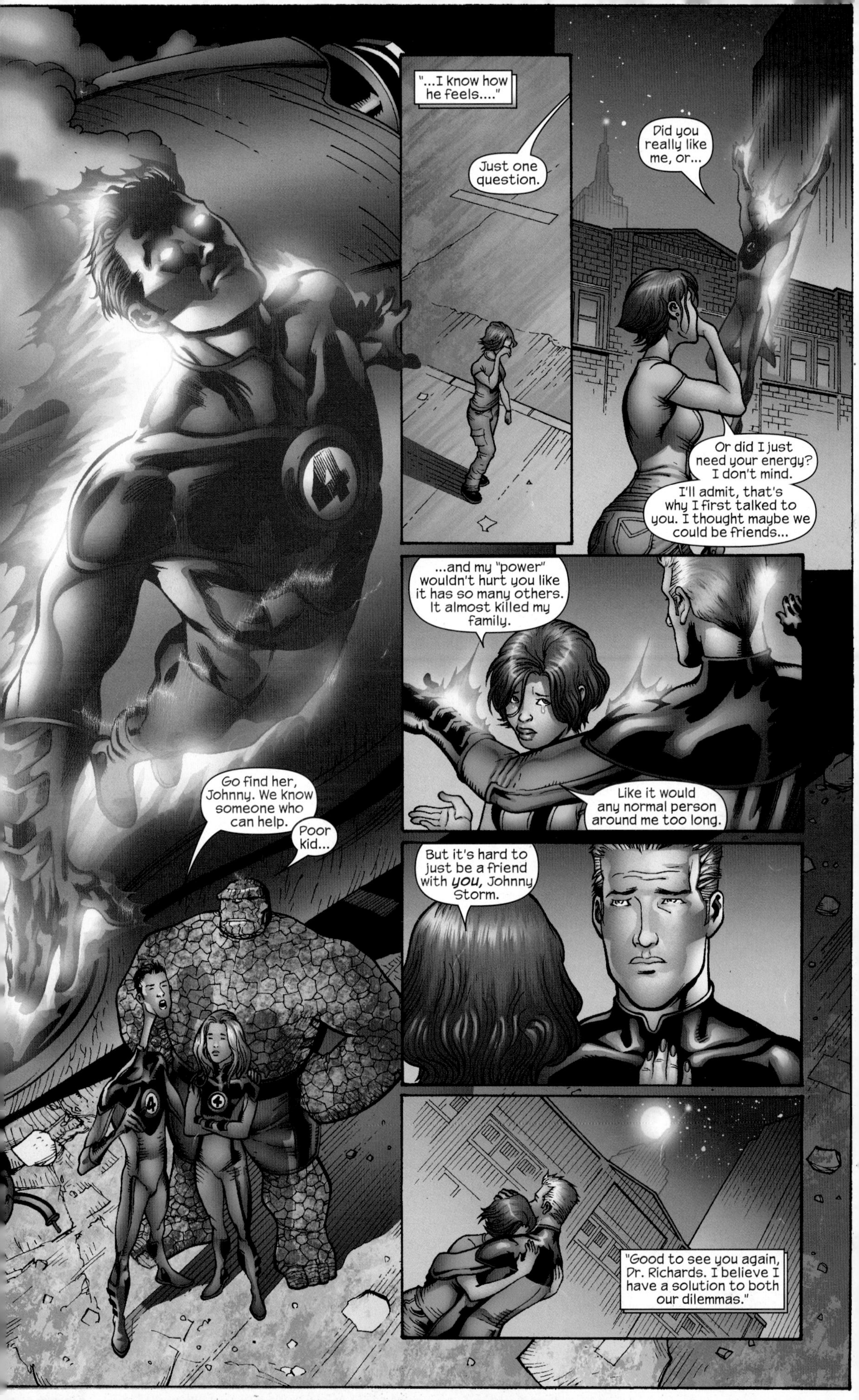
"...I know how he feels...."
Just one question.
Did you really like me, or...
Or did I just need your energy? I don't mind.
I'll admit, that's why I first talked to you. I thought maybe we could be friends...
...and my "power" wouldn't hurt you like it has so many others. It almost killed my family.
Like it would any normal person around me too long.
But it's hard to just be a friend with *you,* Johnny Storm.
Go find her, Johnny. We know someone who can help.
Poor kid...
"Good to see you again, Dr. Richards. I believe I have a solution to both our dilemmas."

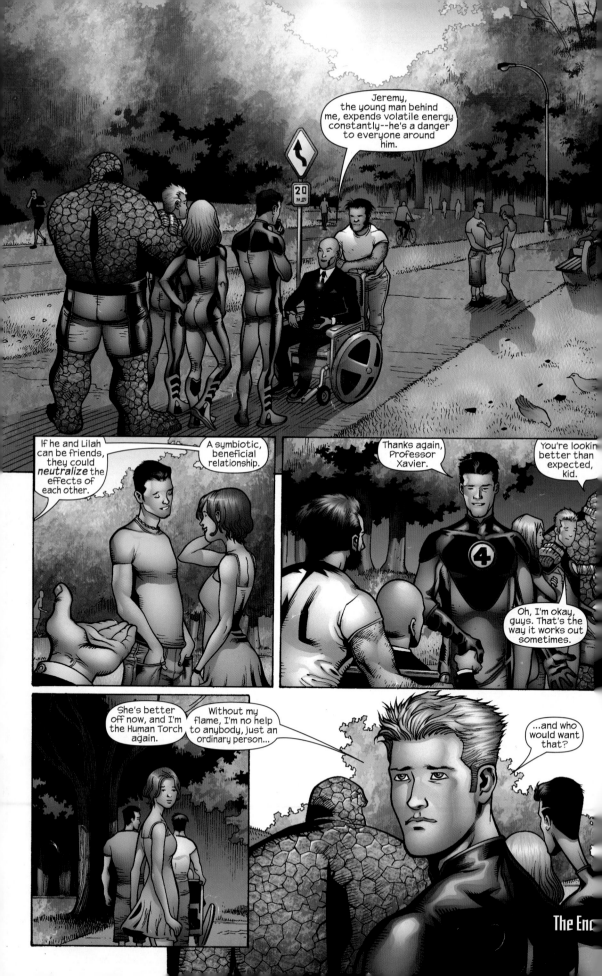

Jeremy, the young man behind me, expends volatile energy constantly--he's a danger to everyone around him.

If he and Lilah can be friends, they could *neutralize* the effects of each other.

A symbiotic, beneficial relationship.

Thanks again, Professor Xavier.

You're lookin better than expected, kid.

Oh, I'm okay, guys. That's the way it works out sometimes.

She's better off now, and I'm the Human Torch again.

Without my flame, I'm no help to anybody, just an ordinary person...

...and who would want that?

The End